The Story of Hula

Written and Illustrated by
Carla Golembe

3565 Harding Avenue
Honolulu, Hawai'i 96816
phone: (808) 734-7159
fax: (808) 732-3627
http://www.besspress.com

For Pam, Ron, and Nora Meek

Mahalo to

Kumu Hula Manu Ikaika and Hālau Hoʻomau I ka Wai Ola ʻO Hawaiʻi, Phyllis Naylor,
Marguerite Murray, and Peggy Thompson, and, always, Joe

*C*ome, *keiki*, and I will show you a treasure.

It is as bright as any star,

more precious than gold or jewels.

My mother gave it to me.

Her father gave it to her.

This gift has been handed down

from generation to generation

since the olden days.

Today I'll share it with you.

It is the treasure of *hula*.

"E Kumu, beloved teacher, what is *hula*?"

Now, that is quite a story . . .

Have you ever sat by the edge of the sea and felt the beating of the waves,

gently lapping at the edge of the sand or pounding against the land?

Come, listen. These are the drumbeats of *hula*.

Do you ever feel like singing when you see a flower bloom?

Has your heart filled with song at the magic of the moon?

Come, sing. This is the chant of *hula*.

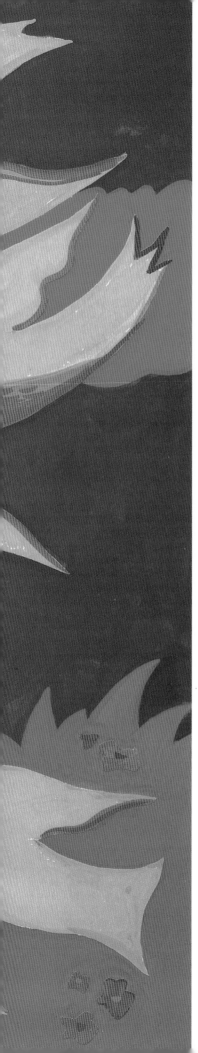

Do you ever watch the birds as they fly
and do they make you want to dance
with your face toward the sky?
Come, dance. This is the dance of *hula*.

"Is *hula* a dance or is it a song?
And can we dance and sing along?"

ipu

ipu heke

pahu

ili 'ili

Hula is the dance of the Hawaiians of old,

still danced today.

But it is much more than a dance.

Long ago, Hawaiians told their tales with

chants.

And just as pictures go with words,

the chants are partners with dance.

Come travel back in time with me.

Can you hear the *mele*,

ancient chanted poetry?

Hear the rattle of the bamboo *pū'ili*

and the click of the *'ili'ili*.

These are the rhythms of *hula*.

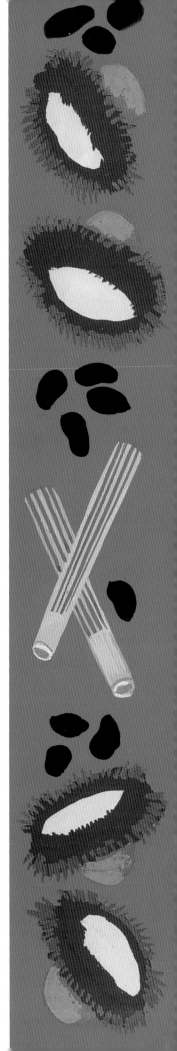

"What are these flowers and leaves in our hair?
And when we dance, what do we wear?"

Your *lei* are made of *kukui* nuts
and flowers that smell sweet.
The shells around your ankles
softly rattle as you move your feet.
Your *pāʻū* are made from *kapa*
or from leaves of ti.
Keiki, you look wonderful,
you're almost ready for the dance.

"We're wearing the costumes of *hula*."

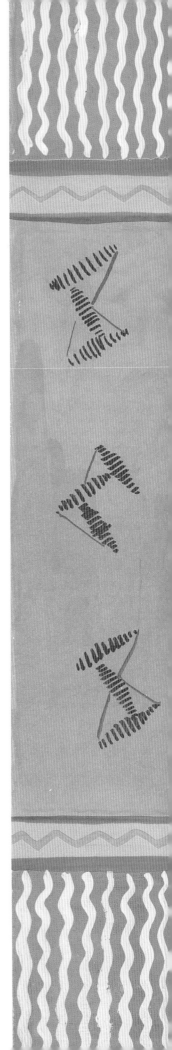

'uwehe

kāholo

"I feel the beat, but what are the steps?

Tell us, e Kumu, what happens next?"

Let your knees bend as you step right then left,

raise your heels and tap them down.

huli   *'ami*

hula kuolo

Turn toward the mountains, turn back toward the sea,

roll your hips around and around. *Kāholo, 'uwehe, huli, 'ami.*

If you practice you'll learn. Some *hula* are danced while the dancer sits.

These are the steps of *hula.*

"Tell us, Teacher, about the chants.

What are we saying as we dance?"

Mele are like poetry. Each *mele* tells a story.

This one tells of a fisherman's wish

that he might find the right place to fish.

Ku'u hālau wa'a i Makanoni

Pae i ke ko'a i Pōhakuloa

Ka ihu o ku'u wa'a i 'Iole'au

I ka hope kai e.

My canoe shed is at Makanoni

The canoe goes to the fishing ground at

Pōhakuloa

The prow of my canoe must turn toward

'Iole'au

The stern toward the open sea.

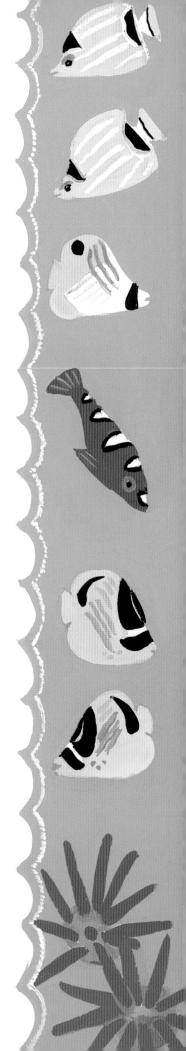

Come dance around the fire

as you chant the *mele*

for the volcano goddess,

whose name is Pele.

She rules the realm

of trembling earth

and hissing flame,

and many ancient *hula*

are danced in Pele's name.

Her legends are legends of *hula*.

Now your feet are dancing

and you can sing the chants.

But the way to tell the story

is with the movement of your hands.

Raise your arms in praise of the *ali'i,*

the kings and queens of old Hawai'i.

Tell stories of their victories, the living, dancing histories.

Their tales are the tales of *hula.*

Pick a flower, string a *lei*, dance the dawning of the day.

Swim like *honu*

as you glide

through quiet waters

side by side.

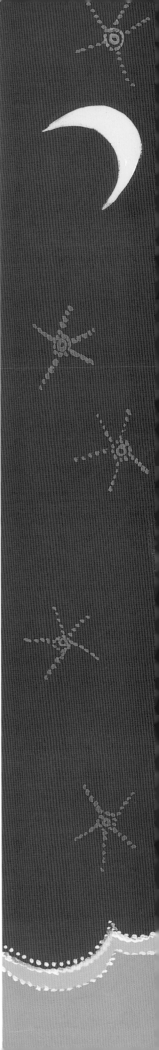

Let your fingers bring down
afternoon rain,
and with the passing of the storm
your hands will tell the story
of a rainbow being born.
These are stories of *hula*.

Your hands can describe a face or a place.
Hula is the balance of strength and grace.
This is the drama of *hula*.

"E Kumu, Teacher, what of today?
Do people still *hula* in the same way?"

When people began to travel the world
they came from near and far.
They introduced melodies, *'ukulele,* and guitar.
Some came from the East
and some from the West.
They brought Hawaiians writing
and different forms of dress.
But though the music and clothing changed,
the power of story remains the same.
And that is the power of *hula*.

The place to learn the *hula* is called the *hālau*. Come, *keiki*, we'll visit mine now.

The *kumu* and the aunties will share the dance and chants and history.

You can play the *'ukulele*. Come, join the *hula* family.

'A'a i ka hula, dare to dance. *Aloha* spirit is all you need to start.

You can come from anywhere if you feel Hawai'i in your heart.

"And that is the magic and that is the joy and that is the story of *hula*!"

Glossary

a hui hou   until we meet again

ali'i   chiefs, royalty

aloha   hello, goodbye, love, and spirit that comes from the heart

'ami   circular movement of the hips

hālau   *hula* school

honu   green sea turtle

hula   the storytelling dance of Hawai'i

hula 'auana   modern-style *hula*

hula kahiko   ancient-style *hula*

hula kuahu   *hula* taught with ceremonies and an altar

hula kuolo   seated chant dance, with gourd drum

hula noho   *hula* danced in a seated position

hula Pele   *hula* dedicated to Pele

huli   to turn

'ili'ili   river rocks held in the hands and used like castanets

ipu   drum made from a gourd

kāholo   *hula* step

kapa   tapa, cloth made from bark

keiki   children

kumu hula   dance master

mahalo   thank you

mele   song, chant

'ohana   family

pahu   large wooden drum

pā'ū   skirt

Pele   fire goddess

pū'ili   split-ended bamboo dancing stick

ti   a native Hawaiian plant with leaves used to wrap food and make clothing

'ukulele   musical instrument used to accompany modern *hula*

'uwehe   *hula* step

Historic Notes

The ancient Hawaiians did not have a written language. They had what is called an oral tradition: all their stories and histories were told through chants and movement, including *hula*.

The *po'e hula,* or *hula* people, performed *hula* for the *ali'i,* the chiefs and chiefesses who were thought to be descendants of the gods. It was not easy to become a *po'e hula.* Each student went through long, disciplined training. Since *hula* is connected to all aspects of life, a student did not study just dance and chanting. To study *hula* was to become aware of history, nature, language, religion, and culture. In the fabric of Hawaiian life, *hula* was the thread.

The place where the *kumu hula* taught was called a *hālau hula.* Each *hālau hula* had an altar, dedicated to Laka, the goddess of *hula.*

The missionaries, who arrived in Hawai'i in 1820, thought that *hula* was immoral. Soon the *hula* was forbidden. But out in the country districts, people kept the art of *hula* alive. They taught and practiced *hula* in secret. It is from these *po'e hula* that the traditional *hula* of the late nineteenth century, which some people call "ancient *hula,*" was handed down.

For the next hundred years or so, acceptance and disapproval of *hula* ebbed and flowed. King Kalākaua encouraged a revival of *hula,* and during the 1880s and 1890s, *hula* was performed publicly. But by 1900, when Hawai'i became a territory of the United States, *hula* seemed in danger of being lost forever.

Hula did survive, but it went through some very big changes. Some people saw *hula* only as entertainment. Melodic tunes replaced the chants. Guitars and *'ukulele* replaced the gourds and drums.

Through most of the twentieth century, non-Hawaiians were familiar with only this kind of *hula.* *Hula* girls performed in stage shows and in Hollywood movies. But the *po'e hula* once again kept the traditional forms alive, and the *kumu hula* continued to teach.

Today people all over the world dance *hula.* It is a form of entertainment, but it is also a way for Hawaiians and non-Hawaiians to learn about the spirit and cultural traditions of Hawai'i. Now *hālau* often teach two kinds of *hula*: the ancient style, which is called *hula kahiko,* and the modern style, called *hula 'auana.*

About the Author/Illustrator

Award-winning children's book author and illustrator Carla Golembe lives in Rockville, Maryland, with her husband, Joe Eudovich, and their two cats, Zippy and Zoe. A student of *hula,* she has visited the islands of Hawai'i, Kaua'i, and Maui to paint, write, and teach.

Design: Carol Colbath

Library of Congress Cataloging-in-Publication Data

Golembe, Carla.
The story of hula / Carla Golembe ;
illustrated by Carla Golembe.
p.   cm.
Includes illustrations, glossary.
ISBN 1-57306-185-9
ISBN 978-1-57306-185-8
1. Hula (Dance) - Juvenile literature.
2. Hula (Dance) - History - Juvenile
literature. I. Title.
GV179.6.H8.G65 2004   793.3199-dc21

Copyright © 2004 by Bess Press, Inc.

The chant (Hawaiian translation by Mary Kawena Pukui, *'okina and kahakō* added) on page 17 is from
Hula: Historical Perspectives, by Dorothy B. Barrère, Mary Kawena Pukui, and Marion Kelly
(Honolulu: Bishop Museum Pacific Anthropological Records Number 30, 1980), page 81.

ALL RIGHTS RESERVED
No part of this book may be reproduced or transmitted in any form by any means, electronic or
mechanical, including photocopying and recording, or by any information storage or retrieval system,
without permission in writing from the copyright holder.

Printed in China

CD recorded at Rendez-Vous Recording.
Performers: Noelani K. Mahoe and Allison Chu.
Fifth printing 2011

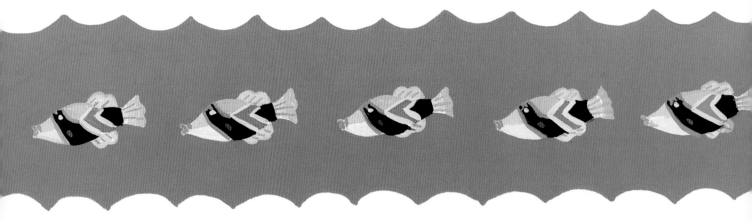